THE INNOCENCE DEVICE

OTHER BOOKS BY WILLIAM KOWALSKI

Novels

Eddie's Bastard (1999)

Somewhere South of Here (2001)

The Adventures of Flash Jackson (2003)

The Good Neighbor (2004)

The Hundred Hearts (2013)

Other titles in the Rapid Reads series

The Barrio Kings (2010)

The Way It Works (2010)

Something Noble (2012)

Just Gone (2013)

THE INNOCENCE DEVICE

WILLIAM KOWALSKI

RAVEN BOOKS
an imprint of
ORCA BOOK PUBLISHERS

Library and Archives Canada Cataloguing in Publication

Kowalski, William, 1970-, author
The innocence device / William Kowalski.
(Rapid Reads)

Issued in print and electronic formats.
ISBN 978-1-4598-0748-8 (pbk.).--ISBN 978-1-4598-0749-5 (pdf).--
ISBN 978-1-4598-0750-1 (epub)

I. Title. II. Series: Rapid reads
PS8571.O985166 2014 C813'.54 C2014-901573-9
C2014-901574-7

First published in the United States, 2014
Library of Congress Control Number: 2014935367

Summary: In a dystopian future where there are only prisoners and those who guard them, a young man survives an uprising and stumbles toward the freedom he's never known. (RL 3.5)

Orca Book Publishers is dedicated to preserving the environment and has printed this book on Forest Stewardship Council® certified paper.

Orca Book Publishers gratefully acknowledges the support for its publishing programs provided by the following agencies: the Government of Canada through the Canada Book Fund and the Canada Council for the Arts, and the Province of British Columbia through the BC Arts Council and the Book Publishing Tax Credit.

Cover design by Jenn Playford
Cover photography by Getty Images

ORCA BOOK PUBLISHERS
PO Box 5626, Stn. B
Victoria, BC Canada
V8R 6S4

ORCA BOOK PUBLISHERS
PO Box 468
Custer, WA USA
98240-0468

www.orcabook.com
Printed and bound in Canada.

17 16 15 14 • 4 3 2 1

To those who have lost their freedom…
…remember that nothing can contain
the human spirit.

ONE

Long ago, in the twenty-first century, when people broke the law and were put in prison, they were kept in cells and not allowed to move about freely. The authorities took away the sunlight, the fresh air, the open spaces. Sometimes they even took away the company of fellow men. The largest of these prisons was called McDowell.

As time passed, more and more laws were made. And more and more laws were broken. More and more people were sent to McDowell. Soon there were too many prisoners. They could no longer be kept in cells. There was simply no more room.

So the jailers of JustiCorps, the guardians of good, decided to show mercy. They built The Wall around the prison and released the inmates to wander around inside. The inmates were still prisoners, still the property of JustiCorps. But now they could live more like those on the outside. They could breathe the fresh air, and they could feel the sunshine.

At first they thought this meant they were free. But if they came too close to the Wall, they were shot. They learned to stay back. And they learned that their freedom was a relative thing.

Over time more and more prisoners came to McDowell, until things got to be the way they are now. These days, most men in the world are in McDowell or places just like it. This is because almost everything is illegal. Talking back to a policeman gets you five years. Any kind of drugs gets you twenty, easy. Drinking and driving means life.

Someone has to guard all these prisoners, which means most of the guards are women.

It's been this way for a very long time. No one remembers anything else.

Inside The Wall, the prisoners made a city, because making cities is what people do. And because JustiCorps is good and merciful, they allowed this to happen.

The year is now 2147. Today, as the early-morning sun comes up, the city the prisoners have made stretches in all directions, as far as the eye can see. The great Wall runs around it. Too high to climb over, too dangerous to approach. There are towers every hundred yards. The Wall is so big and has been there so long that no one even thinks about it, just as they don't think about the air they breathe or the ground they walk on. No one even remembers what is outside. Outside The Wall, the world doesn't exist.

* * *

The prison city of McDowell seems to fill the entire valley. There are many thousands upon thousands of houses. All of them are one-story high. They're made of scraps of wood, clanging sheet metal or flapping pieces of plastic tarp. They lean shoulder to shoulder, like judgmental aunties at a wedding. Sometimes they collapse. Sometimes they burst into flame. Hundreds of prisoners die. Their loss seems to make no difference. There are always more prisoners to take their place.

The lanes between the houses are dusty and filthy. Children of prisoners run up and down, even at this early hour. Raw sewage trickles through ditches. Chickens and goats cry out for food. Dust rises. The city stinks. People are born, suffer and die. There's a kind of order in the chaos. But it disappears as soon as one looks for it, the way a faint star system can be seen only out of the corner of your eye.

The day will be hot again. Every day is hot now. Hotter weather means less food. All over the world, crops are failing. Water is disappearing. Less food means more crime. More crime means more prisoners. But now, even with all the space inside The Wall, there is nowhere to put them. The prison city is already filled to bursting. There will be trouble very soon. Things cannot hold as they are.

In the middle of all this chaos is the old prison building. It rises above the city like a castle, throwing a shadow over the houses that surround it. This shadow is the only cool place in the valley. And it's the only thing that everyone gets to share for free.

Everything else—food, water, firewood, clean air—has a price.

In the old days, the prison building was where all prisoners were kept. Now only the most rich and powerful live inside the cells, away from the heat and dust and noise—and far away from The Wall, symbol of their imprisonment.

Krios, the highest-ranking prisoner, lives here. So do many of his minions. If the rest of the city is a ghetto, the old prison building is a palace. Only those with money can afford it. Privilege radiates outward from the center, the way water ripples after a stone is thrown. The closer you are to the center, the more you have to lose. For this reason, some people like being on the outside.

***

Chago is one of those who lives far from the center of things. He lives near The Wall, where nothing of importance happens. His life is quiet. Nobody knows his name. He's safe. He owns nothing. But he prefers it that way, because it means he has nothing to lose. He is left alone. In some ways, he is as free as it's possible for a prisoner to be.

Chago's house is not really a house. It's a large box. A stiff breeze would blow it over, if there ever was any breeze. It has no windows, no pictures on the walls, no luxuries of any kind. Wood pallets on the floor support his rag mattress. A rough table stands against one wall. Two plastic five-gallon buckets sit by the entry. These are all he owns. There is nothing to do in this house except sit or sleep, so he spends as little time here as possible.

Chago spends a lot of time waiting in lines. When he needs water, he walks to the pump with his buckets and waits his turn to fill them. When he needs food, he stands in another line for hours, waiting for his ration. He was given a hot plate by

JustiCorps, because JustiCorps is good and merciful. But that only works when there is electricity. Electricity is a luxury reserved for the wealthier prisoners. Chago has never used his hot plate.

Instead, there is a small hearth where Chago can cook—when he can afford firewood. The smoke is supposed to go up through a hole in the roof. Usually it just swirls around and goes into his lungs. Chago is only twenty-four, but already he has the cough of an old man.

If his ration doesn't come, and if he has a little money, Chago might buy some food from one of Krios's men. Krios controls most of the food sales in the city. This is why he is so rich.

But if he has no money, Chago sleeps hungry. JustiCorps is supposed to feed all the prisoners three times a day. That has never happened. There are a lot of things that are supposed to happen here and don't.

And there are many things that shouldn't happen and do.

But you don't complain, because JustiCorps is good and merciful. And if you are heard complaining, you might get sent to Gratitude Training.

No one ever comes back from Gratitude Training.

JustiCorps is good and merciful.

Chago gets up this morning before the sun comes over the mountains. He blows last night's coals into life. There are a few precious sticks of wood left from the last bundle. He breaks these up into little pieces and drops them on the coals. Then he boils water and adds heaping spoons of coffee grounds to the pot.

He got these grounds from the garbage of a wealthy prisoner. They have already been used, so he must let them sit in the hot water for a long time. Then he filters the coffee into an old mug.

For his breakfast, he cracks a hard-boiled egg on the table. He rolls it back and forth, feeling the shell crunch under his palm. He picks the bits of shell off and saves them in a can. JustiCorps requires that he do this. When the can is full of eggshells, he will give it to a guard. The guard will give it to the Dirt Department. The Dirt Department will give it to the farmers. The farmers will turn it into compost and use it to grow food. Some of that food will be used to feed chickens. The chickens will lay eggs, and Chago will be allowed to buy them. JustiCorps tells the prisoners that this is the Cycle of Life™, and that they invented it. If you fail to observe the Cycle of Life™, you are in violation. That means another ten years on your sentence, easy.

He eats the egg in mouse-sized bites to make it last longer. Between bites, he takes a mouthful of coffee. As he eats and sips, he stares blankly out the door of his house. People pass his doorway, averting their eyes. It's considered very bad manners to look into someone's home, even by accident. Fights break out over this all the time. Often they are fatal.

It seems the whole city is out and about this morning. Out here, so close to The Wall, everyone is poor. Their clothes are little better than rags. Men and women walk by. Many of these women are free, but they live here anyway with their men. They are carrying buckets of water, live chickens, bundles of sticks, baskets of food. Some of them carry machetes to protect themselves. That's because the things they carry are all they own in the world. There are plenty of hungry people here who will kill you for your things or die trying. They have nothing to lose.

Chago thinks about nothing as he eats. He has nothing to think about. Well, there is one thing—one bright spot in his mind that is so special to him, he dares not visit it. He's afraid that if he thinks about it too much, it will be taken away from him. And that would destroy him. So he forces himself to forget about it for today. He keeps his mind blank.

There is only the day stretching before him, filled with meaningless labor. When he's done with his breakfast, he wipes his mug clean on a rag. He folds the rag neatly and places it on the table. He stops and checks himself in the shard of polished metal he uses as a mirror. He frowns at his close-cropped hair, his dark skin, his thin face, his eyes that seem too pathetic. He would like to look tougher. If the world could see inside him, they would see what kind of person he really is. And they would destroy him in a moment. So he must be sure that never happens.

Then he pulls a curtain across the doorway to his house and leaves for work.

TWO

The lanes between the houses give way to larger avenues. There are four of them, leading outward from the old prison at the center. They are called North, South, East and West. They divide the city into quadrants. On a map, the quadrants look like pieces of a big pie. Each one is under the control of a different boss. Each boss is under the control of Krios. And Krios is under the control of the Warden, whom no one ever sees.

Chago lives near the far end of West Avenue. On his way to work, he walks past endless shanties and lean-tos, all as rickety and shoddy as the one he lives in. No one this close to The Wall has any money.

As he passes each shanty, he keeps his eyes down. Looking in someone's door is asking for trouble. Meeting someone's eyes directly is trouble too. Someone might think he was trying to challenge them.

People have become more and more like animals lately. He doesn't remember it being like this until very recently. It's because there are so many prisoners now. Overcrowding. Everyone is tense. Waiting for something to happen.

There are more guards than ever too. They stand on every corner, wearing black uniforms and earpieces. They wear no guns, for fear a prisoner will take them. But the earpieces allow them to call in the airships at a moment's notice. And if an airship comes, you've got big problems.

Chago knows not to look at the guards. If you stare at them, you're going to have trouble.

As long as he remembers to keep his eyes down, things will be fine.

He comes to West Avenue. As usual, it's thronged with people—men who are prisoners, women who are their wives, children of every size and shape and color. Chago can't believe how crowded the city has become. He can barely move.

Here, out of the neighborhoods, the rules are different. People can talk freely without offending anyone. It's safe to look around. The avenue is lined with stalls selling every kind of food or clothing item or performing nearly every kind of service. Most of them are owned by JustiCorps, and they charge a small fortune for everything. But a few prisoners are allowed to own their own businesses. These are controlled by Krios. What money there is in the city flows to and from him. Mostly to.

Chago arrives at a certain nondescript building on the avenue. He goes in the main door and puts on a smock. Dozens of other men are already there, getting ready for work. He steps inside a room filled with long, high workbenches.

On each bench are models of buildings. The buildings are of two types. One type is a tall tower that looks like a spike. This is a model of a famous building in France. The other is a pyramid, which Chago knows is in a place called Egypt. The bottom of every piece is stamped with the same words: *HANDMADE BY LOCAL ARTISANS*.

Once, Chago asked his friend Binny what a local artisan was.

"You're a local artisan," Binny replied.

Chago could tell he was joking, but he also could tell Binny didn't want him to ask any more questions. He's lucky to work here. His talent got him this job. Lots of prisoners have far worse jobs than this. They work in the mines or the factories, where accidents are common. Nobody lives very long there.

Binny is already here, bent over his table with his paintbrush. When he sees Chago, he smiles. They don't speak. They've known each other for a long time, and there's nothing left to say.

Binny is much older than Chago. He has fluffy gray hair, a gray beard and wrinkles that nearly hide his eyes. He's been a prisoner since he was a child. He doesn't even remember why he was first arrested all those years ago.

Chago doesn't remember why he was arrested either. He has always been a prisoner. He belongs to JustiCorps now. So does Binny. So do all the prisoners in the city. So does the tall tower in France and the pyramid in Egypt. So does the Cycle of Life™. JustiCorps owns everything.

Chago smiles back and picks up his brush. He begins to paint bricks onto one of the pyramids. These little buildings will be shipped away and sold to tourists who are visiting the places that JustiCorps owns. Binny has told him this. Chago is not sure why a person would go somewhere just to see a building. But he doesn't ask questions. He just paints.

They work silently through the morning. Dozens of prisoners, all painting, not speaking, not even looking up. The guards at the front of the room watch them like predators.

Then a call comes over the intercom.

"16505!"

Chago tenses instantly. That has been his number for more than half his life. When he hears it, he freezes.

"16505, report to the front."

Chago dares a glance at Binny. Binny's face is neutral. No sense worrying until you know what you're worried about, he seems to say.

Chago puts his brush in a jar of turpentine and takes off his smock. He goes to the front of the room, where three guards always stand, their eyes roving over the room.

"16505," he says.

"Visitation," says the head guard, a tall blond woman with short hair.

Chago tries to hide his surprise. Today is not Visitation Day. There must be a mistake. But he's not going to say anything. He learned long ago to accept in silence whatever little gifts life throws his way. If no one knows he has them, then no one can take them away.

He hurries out of the workshop and heads for the Visitation Center. He knows he won't have much time. This is the bright spot that is so important to him, he doesn't dare even think about it. He's only allowed to see his son for an hour every three months. He doesn't want to waste a moment of it.

THREE

Chago hurries through the streets. He moves as fast as he can without attracting too much attention. The last thing he wants now is for a guard to stop him and ask a lot of questions. He is not rich or important enough for them to show him any respect. To them, he's just one more scrog.

That's the word they use for people like him—*scrog*. A scrog is a nothing. He has always been a nothing.

But there are two people in this life who thinks he's something. And he is about to spend an hour with them.

So he hurries.

"Hey," says a voice. "Where do you think you're going?"

Chago stops and looks up. He was in such a hurry, he wasn't paying attention. He's almost bumped into a very fat man. The man wears gold necklaces and earrings. His robe hangs open, revealing his plump, hairy belly. His greedy, piglike eyes take Chago in. Behind him stand two other men with large sticks at the ready. This is Blingo, one of Krios's men, and these are his bodyguards.

"I'm sorry," says Chago. He doesn't bother to explain. He just waits.

"Kneel when you talk to me," says Blingo.

Chago kneels in the dust. These are just the things he tries to avoid—trouble and attention. And now he's got plenty of both.

Time passes slowly. He knows Blingo is trying to decide what to do with him.

Have him beaten? Killed? Steal all his belongings? Good luck there. He has nothing worth taking.

And in the end, this is what saves him. Blingo knows he is not worth bothering with. He's just a scrog. Not even worth the trouble it would take to teach him a lesson.

"Get away from me, you filth," says Blingo. "And be more careful around your betters."

"Thank you, boss," says Chago.

He gets up and continues on his way.

The Visitation Center is busy, as usual. At least they don't keep him waiting long. Chago is shown into a room with two chairs in it. Some broken, dirty toys lie in one corner. Weak light trickles from a bulb in the ceiling.

Corazon and Jim-Jim are already there. Corazon is wearing her black guard's uniform. Jim-Jim is sitting on her lap. When he sees Chago, he smiles and holds out his arms. Chago picks him up and hugs him.

"Your knees are dirty," says Corazon.

"Never mind about that. Wasn't expecting to see you so soon," Chago says.

Corazon nods. "He wanted to see you again," she says. "He kept asking for you. So I got us an extra visit."

"He talks now?"

"Quite a lot. Give him time. He'll show you."

"Are you going to let me hear you talk?" Chago asks the little boy.

Jim-Jim is not quite two years old. He stares at his father with his fingers in his mouth.

"You're doing well?" Corazon asks.

Chago nods. He knows it's not a real question. She doesn't much care, and she couldn't do anything about it if she did.

Corazon chose him the way the female guards always choose the fathers of their children. The fact that he was a prisoner was not held against him. It was almost impossible today to find a man who wasn't. But he had no record of violence or disease. She needed someone to make a baby with. If a woman didn't have a baby with a prisoner, she probably wouldn't get to have a baby at all.

But they are not married, and they have no relationship. Chago considers himself lucky he's allowed to see his son. Many prisoners aren't. They know they have children out there somewhere, but they could be anyone. They will never know them. And knowing Jim-Jim brings him a deep sense of joy, like nothing else in his life.

"I'm not doing too bad, for a scrog," he says.

Corazon almost smiles. She's a slim, petite woman with light beige skin who looks good in her black uniform. He can tell by the way she looks at him that there is no longer anything between them. She got the child she wanted. Now she's happy.

But still, she treats him well. For that he is grateful.

"Nice of you to let me see him again," he says. "I never did know what you saw in me."

"You have honest eyes," says Corazon.

"If you think I'm honest, why not get me out of here?"

"You'd just end up right back inside," she says.

"You say that like I'm a criminal."

"If you're not a criminal, then why are you a prisoner?"

"I don't even remember what I did to get sent up in the first place."

"You always say that."

"It's true. I was just a kid when they nabbed me."

"You must have done something."

"I was hungry. I remember that much. So hungry I couldn't think straight."

"How come there are never any guilty people in prison?" Corazon asks.

Chago shrugs. He doesn't want to argue.

He and Jim-Jim play with the toys in the corner for a while. The boy crawls all over him. Chago gets him to say a few words, but *Daddy* isn't one of them. Not yet.

"Thanks for coming," says Chago when the hour is up. A red light over the door comes on to warn them.

"I like to watch you play with him," says Corazon. "It's good for him."

"It's good for me too," says Chago. "Things are crazy around here these days. Too many people."

"I'm being transferred to another sector," Corazon says.

He stares at her.

"You mean another part of the city?"

"No. I mean another city. Like this one."

"I didn't know there was another city like this one."

She looks at him like she almost feels sorry for him.

"The whole world is like this, Chago," she says. "Prison cities everywhere."

"All owned by JustiCorps?"

"Who else?"

He knows she must be right. She is free. She has access to information.

"When are you going?"

"I don't know," she says. "I was going to see about getting you transferred. So you can be near Jim-Jim. They say a boy who knows his father has less chance of going to prison. And I don't want..."

He knows what she's going to say. She feels the same thing he does. They don't want Jim-Jim to end up the property of JustiCorps. But they can't say that out loud. Because JustiCorps is good and merciful.

Transferring would mean leaving behind the only home he's ever known. His little house, his job in the workshop, Binny. It would mean starting over completely. But if it means staying close to Jim-Jim, he won't even think twice about it.

"I want to go too," he says.

Corazon nods.

"I'll let you know," she says.

She reaches out and takes his hand for a minute. Jim-Jim makes a cooing noise. Chago kisses him on the head. Then he walks out of the room. It's like ripping off a bandage. He has to take his leave quickly or he will never do it.

FOUR

It's the next day. Binny and Chago are back at work. Once again they simply look at each other and smile. Then they paint in silence.

Chago loves to paint. It was Binny who taught him how, a long time ago.

"If you want to stay out of the mines or the factories, boy," he had said, "you better learn a skill. Here. This is a paintbrush. This is how you use it."

Chago knows he probably owes Binny his life. Nobody lasts very long in the mines or factories.

Before the midday break, there comes another announcement.

"All prisoners to the screens," says a voice over the PA system. "This is a city-wide order. All prisoners to the screens."

Binny and Chago put their brushes into jars of turpentine and take their smocks off. They line up with the other prisoners and file neatly out of the workshop. Outside they join a massive line that has already formed and is heading for the center of the city. No one speaks. The avenue is lined with guards. They look very serious.

"Something's up," Chago whispers to Binny.

Binny looks at him out of the corner of his eye. Be quiet, his eyes command him.

So Chago stays quiet. He always listens to Binny, because Binny always knows what to do.

They soon arrive at one of the many massive screens that dominate the avenues.

These screens are how JustiCorps' rulers talk to the prisoners. They never actually enter the prison city. That's the job of the guards. But sometimes they hand down new rules or announce new policies. When they do, it's always over the screens. And it's never good news.

The whole population of the city has turned out. No one is allowed to miss an announcement. To do so means getting time added on to your sentence.

They wait, and wait, and wait. The crowd is huge and growing impatient. Finally, the screen flickers into life. A face appears. Chago hasn't seen him in a while. It's the Warden. He looks old.

"Good day, inmates of McDowell City," he says. "This is Warden Pickett speaking."

Chago and Binny exchange glances. If the Warden himself is talking to them, something big is happening.

"No doubt you have noticed that our city is becoming more and more popular," says the Warden. "This is because things are run so well here. Our reputation is sky-high."

Chago looks down at the ground so his eyes don't get him into trouble. He can't stand the lies they are told by those in charge. No one else can either. But no one can do anything about it.

"Here at JustiCorps, the well-being of our inmates is our highest priority."

Chago tries not to laugh. So do the other prisoners. The guards are on high alert. They're just waiting to arrest someone for causing a disturbance. That will get him another three years, easy. They step closer to the crowd of prisoners. Chago can feel their presence. He ignores them, as he has trained himself to do. Someone else nearby, probably a new prisoner, cannot hold his laughter in. There is a commotion as he is hauled away by guards. Chago doesn't dare look. He knows that's probably the last time that man will ever laugh in his life.

"We have so many prisoners on death row, we can't keep up with the executions. We've come up with a new method that we hope will relieve the backlog. But this isn't just a new way of delivering punishment. It does much more than that. In fact, it can make you a free man. We call it the Innocence Device."

So it's to be a public execution. Chago is surprised. They haven't been doing those lately. He wonders what has changed. He hates executions. They make him sick to his stomach. But if they tell you to watch, you watch.

The Warden steps back from the camera, and a strange object fills the screen. It looks like a metal hoop standing on end. It's about seven feet high. That's it. Nothing fancy. And yet there is something strange about it too. It's no ordinary metal. From the way it glows and pulses, it looks to Chago almost as if it's alive.

"The Innocence Device is designed to save years of unnecessary suffering," says the Warden. "Right now, when a man is sentenced to death, he might have to wait a long time for his turn. If he chooses the Innocence Device, he doesn't have to wait another minute. It's fast, efficient and, most of all, painless. All you have to do is walk through the circle.

"But," says the Warden, "that's not all. The Innocence Device is much more than that. It can actually tell whether or not a man is guilty of the crimes he's accused of. We know our justice system isn't perfect. Very rarely, mistakes can be made. The last thing JustiCorps wants is to punish an innocent man. So we are proud to announce this new option for all prisoners. Anyone can decide to do this if they want to.

"If you choose to walk through the Innocence Device, and if it detects your innocence, you will not be executed. Instead, you will be freed from prison immediately and allowed to return to the outside world."

The Warden waits while an excited murmur runs through the whole city. The guards allow it. Even they appear to be astonished by this new development.

"If you're a bad person, of course, you will be executed on the spot," the Warden says. "No matter what your crime." He pauses to let that sink in.

"So how does the Innocence Device know whether a man is innocent or guilty, good or bad? The magic of technology. It can read your entire past with a computer program. It can see everything you've ever done. Let's have a demonstration."

Two men appear on-screen, wearing clothing that marks them as scrogs. One of them is a short, bald, shifty-looking man.

The other is tall and thin and looks terrified. Chago recognizes the tall man right away.

"That's Max the Mincer," he says to Binny.

Max the Mincer is famous. He was once a rich man with a huge family, but he killed all three of his wives and chopped them up into small pieces. Everyone knows about him. He's a celebrity prisoner on death row.

"One of these men is a known murderer, and the other says he is innocent," says the Warden. "They have both volunteered to go through the Innocence Device to show you how it works. The Device will detect their guilt, if it exists, and deal the appropriate punishment. Gentlemen, please go ahead."

The short man looks around nervously. He doesn't seem to want to go through the Device. He looks over his shoulder as if someone is speaking to him. His expression changes to pure terror. Someone is threatening him with something awful. That much is clear.

The short man turns and walks through the Device. Nothing happens. He comes out the other side, looking like a man who's won the lottery on his birthday.

"As you can see, he was not executed," comes the Warden's voice. "So you know what that means. He's a free man now. He can return to the outside world at once."

The short man looks stunned at this information. On the screen, the Warden walks over to him and shakes his hand. He is escorted offscreen by two smiling guards.

Binny and Chago look at each other in disbelief. The crowd is in shock. Can it really be that easy? They are so used to being lied to, it's hard to believe this isn't just another trick. But they just saw it happen before their very eyes. The Warden himself said the short man was free.

"And now our second prisoner will go through the Device," says the Warden.

"I won't," says Max the Mincer, the tall man.

The same two guards reappear on-screen. They aren't smiling now. They each grab one of Max's arms and hold him.

"Everyone knows who you are, and everyone knows what you did," says the Warden. "You admitted it in court. You accepted your sentence of death. It's coming sooner than you thought, that's all. Put him through."

The guards pull Max the Mincer to the Innocence Device. When he begins to scream and fight, two more guards appear. They each grab an arm or leg. Then they heave Max through the Device like a bag of potatoes.

There is a flash of light. Max the Mincer falls to the ground. He doesn't move. A wisp of smoke hovers above him. A doctor appears on-screen and takes his pulse.

"Dead," he announces.

There is a cheer from the crowd. No one had liked Max the Mincer very much.

"As you can see, it works perfectly," says the Warden, reappearing on-screen. "Today, we will be installing several Innocence Devices around the city. Tomorrow will be a holiday. No one works. Anyone can choose to go through a Device, anytime they want. If the device determines you are an immoral person, you will be executed on the spot. If you are moral, you will be set free. Either way, the Innocence Device will bring an end to your suffering immediately. So what are you waiting for?"

There is another cheer from the crowd. Guards with fierce expressions and busy cattle prods ensure the cheering goes on for a long time.

"JustiCorps," says the Warden, "is good and merciful."

FIVE

After the announcement, they are given the rest of the day off. Chago and Binny go back to Chago's house. Binny sits in silence while Chago makes him a cup of coffee. He uses the same grounds from this morning. He pours a mug for Binny and sits down with the pot on the dirt floor before him. When the pot is cool enough, he drinks from it. He only has one mug. His guest should have it.

"I wonder how bad you have to be before that thing will zap you," says Chago. "Can it see everything you've done in your life?"

"That's what the Warden said."

"How does it work?"

"Computers," says Binny.

"How can a computer know if you're bad? It doesn't make sense."

"People ain't here because they're bad."

"What do you mean? This is a prison. It's where bad people go."

"Do you think you're a bad person?"

"Not really," says Chago.

"Then what are you doing here?"

"I dunno. I don't remember anything else. It's all some kinda mistake. But here I am."

"Right. Here you are. People are here because they're here. That's all. You get swooped up in a raid, you get sent off, you never see your people again, and every time you screw up they just keep adding on to your sentence."

"But why?" says Chago.

"What do you mean, why? For the money."

"What money?"

Binny looks at him.

"JustiCorps gets money from the government," he says. "You didn't know that?"

Chago stares.

"For every person locked up in here, they get thousands of dollars a year. You and me, we're no good to anyone if we're free. We're not making anyone any money. In here, we bring in money for the owners."

"What owners?"

"The people who own JustiCorps," says Binny patiently.

Chago tries to understand this. He has never thought of JustiCorps as a business, like one of the food stalls in the city center. He's thought of it as a fact of life, like the sky. The idea that it could be owned by somebody is new to him.

"So who owns it?"

"Rich people. Politicians," says Binny. "The same politicians who make the laws that put us here in the first place."

Chago feels his head spinning. It's all too much to take in. First Corazon tells him she is going to another city and taking Jim-Jim. Then she says she wants to bring him along. He hasn't even told Binny that part yet. Then the Warden introduces the Innocence Device. And now Binny is telling him his whole world is owned by a few fat cats who have rigged the system against him purely for their own profit.

So he returns to the most obvious thing, because he doesn't know what else to say.

"I still don't see how a machine can tell if a man is guilty or not," he says.

"Me neither," says Binny.

"How can a computer program know what you've done?"

"I don't know."

"And what if it's wrong?" Chago says.

Binny shrugs.

"Well, I ain't going through that thing," Chago says.

"I am," says Binny.

Chago looks at him in surprise. Binny is the last person he would have expected to try the Innocence Device.

"You what?"

"Yeah. I'm goin' through."

"But what if it doesn't work right?"

"You saw for yourself," says Binny. "It zapped the bad guy. It let the good guy through. And when it zapped him, it zapped him good. He didn't feel nothin'."

"So?"

"So, even if it's wrong, I won't feel a thing. And if it's right...either way, I'm gonna be free."

"Free, huh?"

Chago doesn't like the look on Binny's face. He's never seen him look this way before. He looks like he's staring at something only he can see. Something far away, and maybe not even real. This is not the Binny he knows. The Binny he knows always has the right answers. This Binny looks like he's living in dreamland.

"What would you do if you got free?"

"I had a sister once," says Binny. "Don't know where she is, but I'd like to find her. I had a family. Some of them might still be around." He looks as if he's just remembered this. "I had a family."

"You always told me you don't remember why you got put away," Chago says.

"That's right. I was just a kid."

"So...you're pretty sure you're innocent, right?"

"You don't think I would remember if I killed somebody? Or robbed a bank? I ain't done nothing to nobody," says Binny. "Fact is, I don't think I ever did anything in the first place. I think I just got swept up because I was poor. I never had a trial. I just got sent here. This is my one chance to prove I'm innocent. That I'm a good person. I'll never get another shot besides this."

Chago ponders all this. It's craziness. His whole life has been turned upside down in a matter of a few hours.

"When are you going through?"

"Tomorrow," says Binny. "First thing."

SIX

Chago lies awake all night. When the sun comes up he walks to Binny's house and meets him. With their customary silence, they head down West Avenue. There, ahead of them, they see a long line of people.

"What's that for?" Chago asks.

"They're going through the Innocence Device," says Binny. "Everybody wants to be free."

"All those people?" says Chago. There are thousands of them. The line is not moving. He can't even see the front of it.

They join the line at the end.

Binny asks the man in front of them, "You going through?"

The man nods. "We'll be waiting here all day. Maybe longer. But we'll get there. And once I get through that thing, I'm gonna be free. I never did anything wrong in the first place."

"Me neither," says Binny.

"You going through?" the man asks Chago.

Chago shakes his head. "I'm just here with my friend," he says.

They wait. The day wears on. The line creeps forward. Behind them, it gets longer. They have brought nothing to eat or drink. Chago hadn't planned on waiting this long. Fights break out as people get impatient. Guards walk up and down. They carry electric prods, and they use them to keep people well-behaved. Some of Krios's men appear, selling food and water. Their prices are ridiculous. Neither Chago nor Binny has any money.

"You should go home," says Binny. "I could be here a long time."

But Chago shakes his head.

"I'm staying," he says.

The line creeps forward. After a while he can hear people at the end making noise. Sometimes they cheer, sometimes they groan. By the end of the day, he is close enough to see what's going on.

The Innocence Device is up on a platform, still far away but high enough to be seen. It has attracted a crowd of people who are just watching. Like it's a game, an entertainment.

As Chago watches, a man walks through. Nothing happens. He raises his arms for joy. A guard shakes his hand and hands him some papers. The crowd cheers for him. He's free.

Three more men walk through and are zapped, one after another. The crowd groans every time. Some of the spectators are betting. Guards are waiting to haul their bodies away. Some of the men in line lose their nerve and turn away. The guards don't seem to like this, but they make no move to stop them. They are not forcing people to go through.

Binny begins to sweat.

"If I don't make it, you can have all that's mine," he says.

"You don't have anything," says Chago.

"That's right," says Binny, smiling one of his rare smiles. "And it's all yours."

"You sure you wanna do this?"

"I'm sure."

"You can still change your mind."

"I don't need to. My mind is made up. I never did nothing to nobody, Chago, you hear me? I never hurt a single person. My only crime is that I'm poor. That's it. You watch. You're gonna see me walk out the other side of that thing a free man."

They're very close now. The Innocence Device appears much larger than Chago realized. This close, it seems alive. The metal shimmers like the skin of a jewel. He can hear a strange hum in the air. It pulses like it's full of energy. The air is full of death and freedom. It's a strange combination.

The man in front of them is tapped on the shoulder.

"Go," says the guard.

The man walks forward slowly. At the last moment he hesitates. The guard shoves him roughly through.

Nothing happens. There is no flash of light. On the other side, it seems to take the man a moment to realize he is free. He laughs with delight. A guard hands him some papers and shakes his hand.

"This is it," says Binny.

Chago wants to say or do something, but he can't move or speak. Binny looks at him for a long moment. He holds out his hand. Chago takes it. They shake.

"See you on the other side," says Binny.

"Sure will," says Chago.

"Move it," says the guard.

Binny steps up to the Device. He takes a deep breath. Then he steps through.

There is a flash of light. The crowd groans.

"Next," says the guard, as they haul his body away.

SEVEN

Chago doesn't remember walking home. He's in a daze. He enters his house and lies on his rag mattress. He's so shocked that for once he doesn't even feel the bedbugs biting him.

When Binny had said he'd never done anything wrong, Chago believed him. And he still does. Binny practically raised him. Chago can't remember a time when he didn't know the kindly, white-haired old man. Binny had never raised a hand to Chago. He didn't even use bad language around him. He was like a father to him.

That made him the only father Chago had ever known.

And now his body lay in a heap of other bodies somewhere. They probably just take them away and burn them in a furnace, Chago thinks. They don't even get a decent burial.

Poor Binny. He had seemed so hopeful.

Chago is exhausted, but he knows he will get no sleep again that night. Every time he closes his eyes, he sees Binny's face. Then he sees Binny lying on the ground, lifeless. A wisp of smoke trails above his body. Part of him knows that smoke was just from the zap that killed him. But another part of him thinks maybe it's Binny's soul escaping his body. Finally free, just like he wanted.

Chago cannot sleep and cannot stay awake. He drifts in and out, staring up at the ceiling, until he hears a strange noise coming from outside.

The noise sounds like something very large and powerful, like a massive machine flattening the earth. And it sounds like it's coming this way.

He gets up and goes outside. It's late at night, and the sky is dark. But in the direction of the city center, the sky is glowing orange.

As he stands in the narrow lane outside his house, other prisoners come out of their houses too. They all stand and listen together. For once they ignore the rule against looking at each other in the neighborhoods.

"What is that?" asks Chago's neighbor, a man who was born in the prison city. He is simply named Twelve.

"I don't know," says Chago.

"It sounds like people," says another neighbor. "A lot of people."

Chago listens more intently. His neighbor is right. The sound he is hearing is not a machine. It's the sound of thousands of voices raised in anger.

It's a riot.

Fear grips him, unlike anything he's ever known. His bowels turn to water. This sound is a vengeful beast that can destroy everything in its path. The earth is about to split open.

And yet, Chago finds he must know what is happening.

He says, "I'm going to check it out."

"Man, are you crazy?" says Twelve. "Those airships will be coming in and shooting up everybody. Last time there was a riot, three thousand people got killed."

But Chago barely hears him. He's already gone.

***

He makes it to West Avenue, and there he stops, for the crowd in the street is too thick to move through. There are no guards in sight. Prisoners are running as if they don't care about the rules anymore. Everyone is headed in the same direction—toward the orange glow at the city center.

Chago feels himself drawn as if by a magnet. He knows the situation is dangerous, but the roar of the mob is intoxicating. He joins the prisoners. He feels like a minnow in a school of fish. He asks the man next to him, "What's going on?"

"The prisoners are taking over the city!" the man tells him.

Chago is electrified. He can't believe what he's hearing. He has never heard those words before. He feels his heart leap in his chest. Suddenly, he feels a thousand pounds lighter.

He's never been in a riot, but he's heard about them. He's excited—he can't believe this is really happening to him. Part of him stands back and watches while the other part runs with the mob. So this is what it's like to be free, he thinks. He feels the crushing boot of authority slip off the back of his neck. For the first time in his life, he feels like he could float away. He's five years old again. The age he was before he came here, before he had ever heard of JustiCorps. He thought he'd forgotten that part of himself. But he had just buried it. It's alive and well inside him.

The mob of which Chago is a tiny part arrives at the city center. The old prison looms above them. Near the prison is another huge structure. This is the Admin Building. It's a ten-story complex of offices and guards' quarters. From here, JustiCorps runs the whole city. If the old prison is a symbol of power and prestige, the complex is a symbol of authority. No prisoner has ever been inside. It's protected by walls of electrified barbed wire.

Now the Admin Building is burning. This is the source of the orange glow.

Flames light up the bottoms of the clouds. But those aren't clouds, Chago realizes. It's the smoke from the fire. It's so big it seems like both earth and sky are aflame.

Fear courses through him. He hopes Corazon and Jim-Jim are okay. He becomes crazy with a desire to know where they are. But he also knows he will never find them in this mad crush of humanity. He can barely move. He is as helpless in the mob as a leaf on a river. There is nothing he can do except try not to trip and fall. If that happens, he knows he will be flattened in an instant.

Above him, a screen flickers to life. The mob stops as one.

"Look!" people yell. "Look at the screen!"

Everyone looks up. Chago is expecting to see the Warden, ordering them all to return to their homes before the airships come to kill them.

But it's not the Warden's face that fills the screen. Instead, it's a sleek-looking man with swept-back silver hair. His expression is one of supreme confidence.

"Krios!" everyone begins to scream. "It's Krios!"

Krios smiles. No doubt he can hear them. Sound goes two ways through the big screens.

"Greetings, my fellow prisoners," he says.

There is a roar as everyone responds.

"So. I have some news for you. The lunatics are no longer running the asylum."

Everyone pauses. What does he mean?

"The city is ours," Krios says. "Mine... and yours. We're in charge now. We're free. Just like we were meant to be."

Mad cheering erupts.

"I'm sorry to say it was all too good to be true. The Innocence Devices were rigged," Krios goes on. "It was just an excuse for the Warden to start killing us off. Well, guess what? His plan didn't work. And tomorrow, my friends, we will see justice, real justice, done here for the first time. Tomorrow, it's the guards who will be going through the Innocence Device. Tomorrow is the first day of the rest of your lives. You are no longer prisoners. Tonight you go to sleep free men!"

The noise that comes from the crowd then is so loud that Chago feels himself go deaf. Around him, everyone else seems to be feeling the same excitement he felt just moments ago. But now he is at a loss to explain the strange feeling that has so suddenly overtaken him. Why does he not feel the same as everyone else? Why isn't he jumping up and down and screaming?

Slowly he worms his way out of the crowd. Everyone is so worked up, they don't even mind if he stomps on their toes.

Finally he arrives at the edge of the mob, and there he stops to look back. The shimmering face of Krios beams over the adoring crowd as the city center burns.

EIGHT

Chago wants to go home, where he feels safe. But he knows if he sits there and stares at the walls any longer, he will go crazy with worry for Jim-Jim. Not to mention Corazon. So he wanders back up West Avenue, trying not to meet anyone's eyes. There is hardly anyone here. The streets are empty. Everyone is at the center. Even the shops are left open and unmanned. He could take what he wants right now. But stealing is wrong. Even from Krios. And it's very dangerous. If he's caught, he will be killed.

Chago sees two men talking on a corner. As he passes, they stare at him. He doesn't look back. Both of them are carrying large automatic rifles. Krios's men.

"Hey," says one.

Chago ignores him.

"Hey!"

He stops.

"Yeah," he says.

There is a long moment of silence.

"Isn't it great to be free?" says the man.

Chago nods.

"Yeah," he says. "Great."

"You don't look happy."

"I'm happy."

"How come you're not downtown with everyone else?" asks the other man.

"Not feeling well," says Chago. "Gotta go home."

"You got papers?" says the first man. "What's your ID number?" They start walking toward him.

"I've got death-row fever," says Chago. "You better stay away from me."

The men freeze and back up.

"I should shoot you right here," says the second man, raising his gun. "Spreading that filth around the city? You know you're supposed to stay in your house until your symptoms are gone."

"I thought we were free now," says Chago. "I thought we could do what we wanted."

He sees their thumbs move as they undo the safeties on their weapons.

Chago turns and runs.

The gunfire spatters on the road behind him as he makes it around a corner. He doesn't stop. He knows they won't come after him. They're too afraid of catching the fatal illness that can wipe out a whole neighborhood in days. But they might remember his face. He'd better be careful for a while.

The guards of JustiCorps would never have just shot me down in the street, he thinks. They would have put me in quarantine. They never killed people for no reason.

He keeps running as fast as he can until he makes it home.

NINE

The next day the word comes down that no guards have been hurt. No children have been harmed. Not yet. Chago feels like sobbing with relief. Jim-Jim is okay.

But then he hears something that makes him feel worse. Krios is holding them all hostage. None of them are allowed to leave the old prison. And the guards are going through the Innocence Device today.

Meanwhile, JustiCorps has gathered a huge force outside the city. But they aren't attacking, because of the hostages. All morning Chago waits for the airships to come and strafe the city with their red-hot bullets. But the skies remain quiet. He wonders what they are waiting for.

He stays in his house. The feeling of dread from last night has only gotten worse. Now that Krios runs the city, his henchmen will be out in force, making sure everyone knows who is in charge. And as much as Chago fears the guards and the wrath of JustiCorps, he fears Krios's men more. At least JustiCorps followed some kind of rules.

Around midday something unthinkable happens. He hears shouting in the neighborhoods. Male voices are raised in anger. There are gunshots. Then, out of nowhere, there is a face in his doorway.

His doorway. His house. His sanctuary, the one place that no one in the whole prison city would ever think of violating. Now a large, hairy man with ammo belts across his chest and a gun in his hand is standing there, already half inside Chago's house without even asking permission. He wears a black armband.

Chago is so shocked, he cannot move. To ignore a taboo this openly speaks either of great stupidity or great power. And he is not about to call this man stupid to his face.

"To the center," the man growls. "Now."

And then he's gone.

Chago steps out of his house, shaking with rage. But he quickly forgets his anger when he sees the horrible sight that greets him. The lane is strewn with bodies. He recognizes Twelve among them.

Meet the new boss, Chago thinks. Worse than the old boss.

He steps over the bodies, trying not to look down.

Once again a tsunami of humanity surges down the avenue. But the mood is very different this time. Everyone senses that the rules have changed. The freedom is gone from the air. Things feel dangerous. There is no talking. Krios's men line the avenue, guns at the ready.

They arrive in the shadow of the old prison once again. The guard complex is now a smoldering ruin. Devilish fumes spiral upward out of the rubble. Tens of thousands of people have gathered. A massive platform has been built overnight. Chago is close enough to see that there are lots of people on it, some of them in guard uniforms. Their hands are tied behind their backs. The others look like Krios's men. All of them wear black armbands.

Then a man steps out into the center of the platform, and Krios's face appears on-screen.

So this is Krios himself, on the platform at the same time as his image is beamed over the city. Chago finds himself fascinated. He has never seen Krios in the flesh before. From here he looks very small. His voice booms out through the PA system.

"Friends," he says, "I've got some good news. All of you who have children by these guards will be glad to know that your sons and daughters will be well treated. They will join us! They will become free citizens of the city, just like you and me!"

A roar of approval. Krios is good, people seem to be thinking. Krios understands us.

"And there's more. Today we are going to see justice served. I gave all the guards a choice: go through the Innocence Device, or take a bullet to the head. The ones you see behind me are the ones who refused to go through. So, guess what? They're about to find out what it means to defy Krios."

As Chago watches, men appear on-screen with guns and point them at the row of terrified guards. The entire crowd falls deathly silent.

Then Chago hears a man yelling at the top of his lungs.

"No!" the man screams. "Wait! Don't do it! This is wrong!"

The man screams so loud that Krios himself appears to have heard him. Chago wonders who would be so stupid as to single himself out for attention.

Then he realizes that the man who yelled was himself.

For he has recognized Corazon among the guards to be executed on the platform. And he cannot let the mother of his child go. Corazon has always said that Jim-Jim needs a father if he is going to stay out of jail. But Chago knows that Jim-Jim needs his mother even more.

"Who was that?" Krios says, shading his eyes and looking over the crowd. "Who's the bleeding heart who thinks these haters of freedom should be treated better than we ever were? Bring him to me."

As if by magic, a circle of empty space has appeared around Chago. He can sense a hundred fingers pointed at him. He feels himself grabbed by the arms and lifted off the ground by very strong men. Before he knows it, he's been carried through the crowd, which parts for him like the waters of the sea spreading for a prophet. More men on the platform reach down and grab him by the shoulders and shirt. They pull him up and march him before Krios.

Chago is surprised to find he is several inches taller than the most powerful man in the city. Krios is a handsome man, well fed, wearing simple but elegant clothes of black. He looks Chago up and down, a smile on his face.

"Which one is yours?" he asks. "I'll send her outside the city. I promise."

Chago is too afraid to answer.

"It's all right," says Krios. "Which one? You don't have to be afraid."

"You...you promise you'll send her out?" says Chago.

Krios nods.

"I promise," he says.

"And our baby?"

"Your baby will be safe."

Chago scans the line of women until he sees Corazon. She's looking down at the ground, numb and terrified.

"There she is," he says, pointing.

Corazon is bundled forward by some other men until she stands before them.

"This is her?" says Krios. "This is the one you want to save?"

"Yes," says Chago.

"Fine," says Krios. He nods to one of his men, who brings his gun up to the back of Corazon's head and fires.

The next several moments feel as if they are happening to someone else. Chago hears himself screaming again.

"No!" he howls. "You lied!"

"I said I would send her out of the city," says Krios. "I didn't say in what condition. You defy me, this is what happens. What if everyone thought they could just do whatever they wanted? We would have total anarchy."

Chago falls to his knees. He is sobbing.

"Get up," says Krios. "Pick her up. Carry her out. Give her to her own people. We don't need all these bodies stinking up the place. Go on. I always keep my word. Take her out of the city, just like I promised."

Chago bends over and picks up Corazon's lifeless form. He has not held her in his arms since before Jim-Jim was born. He's forgotten how soft she is. He never gets to touch soft things. Maybe this is the last time he ever will.

The crowd parts for him again as he climbs down from the platform and heads toward the city gates, Corazon's body in his arms.

TEN

It's the first time Chago has approached these gates in eighteen years. He was only five when he came to the city. Since then his world has been limited to a scant couple of square miles. Now he's about to step outside once again. He's dreamed many times of this moment. But the truth is, it's been so long since he's tasted freedom that he doesn't really remember what it's like. He had stopped expecting it to come.

And if he'd known it would be like this, he wouldn't have wanted it.

The gates swing open as he steps toward them. He tries not to look down at Corazon's empty face. She stares with dead eyes up at the sky. She's heavy and limp in his arms. He can feel her blood soaking his shirt as she grows cool against him. He has often thought of holding her in his arms again. But this, too, he would not have wanted if he'd known how it would be given to him.

The gates close again behind him.

Chago stops and looks around. He's confused. Everywhere, he sees certain things that look familiar—green things, all different sizes, some no taller than his foot, others reaching to his knee. There are thousands of them. Maybe millions. He can't remember what they are or what they are called.

After a moment he remembers—they're plants.

There are so many of them! Dozens of different kinds. Grass underfoot, weeds growing by the road, trees in the distance. All plants. There are no plants growing inside The Wall because there is no space for them to grow. Every square inch is taken up with people or buildings. Everything inside The Wall is brown and gray. Everything outside The Wall is green.

He'd forgotten all about plants. How could he have done a thing like that?

Easy, he thinks. The only vegetables he gets are so old they are practically gray. You can't even tell what they are. They certainly don't look like this—alive and vibrant with color.

This is the color of things in the world, he thinks. This is what things actually look like.

Something else is different too. It's the way the air smells. He sniffs cautiously. There is no stink of raw sewage, of cooking food, of unwashed bodies. The air just smells like...air. He'd forgotten that air has a smell. Maybe this is something he never knew before. He might have been too young to notice things like that. He knows he's better at noticing things now that he's older. He wonders what else he might have noticed in the world if he hadn't been locked up all this time. There are plants, and there is air. What other riches are there?

A road stretches before him. It disappears over a low rise. He turns to look at the city gates. He can see some of Krios's men watching him from the guard towers, but they offer him no hint of what to do. They just stare from their perches like faraway birds who might eat him or might just fly away.

He turns again and takes a few steps down the road. Do they mean for him to just keep walking? He would like nothing better than to put down his burden and leave this place forever. But he can't just drop Corazon in the road. He can't treat her that way. And there is still Jim-Jim to think about.

Just then, in the shimmering haze on the road ahead, he sees something appear. As Chago moves up the small rise, he sees that it is a man in a dark JustiCorps uniform. He wears mirrored sunglasses, so Chago cannot see his eyes.

Chago stops. But the man waves him forward.

Chago obeys. As he tops the rise, he sees an astounding sight: thousands of men and vehicles, all of them heavily armed, just out of range of the view of the city. McDowell is surrounded. JustiCorps' army is waiting to attack.

So, there's more to this world than plants and air. There are men with guns. There are powerful machines of destruction. He should have known.

The man who waved is waiting for him.

"Who are you?" he calls.

"16505," says Chago.

"Who is that you're carrying?"

"Her name is Corazon. She's a guard. The mother of my son, Jim-Jim. He's still in there."

The man stares at him. Or, at least, Chago thinks he is staring at him. He can't see his eyes, so he can't tell. But he can feel them on him all the same, even through the lenses.

"What are you doing here?"

"They told me to bring her out. They want to start getting rid of the bodies."

"How many bodies are there?"

Chago thinks.

"A lot," he says.

"How many is a lot?"

"I don't know how to count very high."

"Are there more than a hundred? Ten tens?"

"Maybe. And there are going to be more very soon."

"Come forward," says the guard.

A white vehicle with a flashing red light rolls up and stops. The rear doors open and two men get out. They're pushing a kind of bed on wheels. Chago lies Corazon on the stretcher. One of the men covers her with a sheet, even her face. In that moment it hits Chago that he will never see her again. They put the rolling bed back in the white vehicle and get in. Slowly it rolls back the way it came.

"How many men does he have?" the JustiCorps officer asks. "How many tens?"

Chago shrugs. "I don't know," he says.

The man stares at him.

"What kind of weapons do they have?"

"Guns."

"Of course, guns. What kind of guns?"

"I don't know."

"Do you want to be free?"

"I am free."

"Who told you you were free?"

"Krios."

"The man who killed this woman? He told you you're free? Well, I guess he can be trusted, can't he?"

Chago says nothing. He sees the man's point.

"Only JustiCorps can make you free," says the officer.

"You? You're the people who locked me up in the first place."

"We can make you free again. But we need you to help us," the man says, as if he hasn't heard. "We need information from you. You're the first person to come out since the riot. We need to know everything you know."

"I don't know anything," says Chago.

The man nods.

"You may think you know nothing," he says. "But you've seen what's going on there. You know how they're deployed. You can help us."

"What's deployed?"

"How they're laid out. Where they're hiding."

"They're not hiding. They're out in plain sight. They own the place."

"Help us get Krios."

"Help JustiCorps?"

The officer says nothing. He just waits.

"You're the people who locked me up when I was five years old," says Chago. "I didn't even do anything wrong. I was just a kid."

The man pulls a piece of equipment out of his pocket and taps at it. He reads it, then frowns.

"16505," he says. "It says here you were a thief. That's why you were locked up."

"I was hungry."

"Then time was added on to your sentence. Talking back. More thievery. Disrespect. Failure to obey lawful orders."

"These are reasons to keep a man in prison for his whole life?"

"Society must be orderly," says the officer.

"Is it true JustiCorps gets money for every prisoner it keeps?"

The officer stares at him for a while longer. His mirrored lenses remind Chago of the backs of spoons.

"You're not going to help us," he says.

"That's right. I'm not going to help you," says Chago.

"Well then, I guess you'd better get back where you belong."

"I thought I was free."

"You're never going to be free. You're a prisoner of JustiCorps. And if you don't get back where you belong, I'll shoot you right here."

Chago feels so many things that he doesn't know which to feel first. He would like to put his hands around this man's neck and squeeze the life out of him. He would like to scream. He would like to just run away over the horizon, until all this nonsense is far behind him and he ends up in a clean, fresh place where he can just be himself, where he can start all over.

But such a place does not exist.

And there is Jim-Jim to think about.

So he turns and heads back for the city.

When he arrives, the gates open for him, and he steps inside without looking back. He walks back into the stench and the noise and the blood.

ELEVEN

Back inside, he sees that the crowd has gone. But Krios is still there, along with several of his men. He's waiting for Chago.

"So. You came back," he says.

"Yes," Chago says. He decides not to explain.

Krios nods. "You had your chance to escape, and you didn't take it. Why is that?"

Chago doesn't answer, because he doesn't know. He waits.

"I'll tell you why I think it is," says Krios. "It's because your heart is here with your brothers. That says a lot about you."

If there's one thing Chago has learned in prison, it's how to keep his mouth shut. Even though Krios is wrong, he doesn't disagree. He just stands there.

"I have room in my group for men like you," says Krios. "I know it wasn't easy for you to carry her out. But it was a test. And you passed. After all, she was just a guard. You're twice the man anyone else here is."

Krios looks around. His henchmen look upset at this statement, but none of them dare talk back. Chago doesn't meet their eyes. He wants no trouble from them later. He's already made them look bad.

"She was a guard," Krios repeats, "and you are a scrog. And once a scrog, always a scrog. Am I right?"

Chago nods. "That's right," he says.

"What would a scrog do on the outside anyway? You don't know what things are like out there. They're bad. Nobody has enough food. There's fighting. Floods.

Trust me, we're better off. They wish they could be in here with us."

Even though he knows Krios lies every time he opens his mouth, Chago can tell he's not lying now. Not when he talks about what it's like out there. Chago did not see these things himself. The world looked like a wonderful place. But it was JustiCorps' world. And he knew he had only seen a tiny piece of it.

"Okay," he says.

"Okay what?"

"You said you had room for me in your group. So can I have a job, please?"

Krios smiles.

"I thought you'd never ask," he says. "Give this man an armband."

***

Hours later, Chago is standing on a corner, in charge of a group of eight men. He doesn't know any of them. They're scrogs, just like him. They are waiting for him to tell them what to do. He has never been in charge of anyone in his life. Krios has told the eight men to obey Chago or they will be killed. Not by Krios. By Chago. With the new gun he's holding.

Chago has never held a gun before. He tries not to let the other men know that he has no idea how to use it. If they could see how useless he is, they wouldn't listen to a word he says. He has no intention of killing anyone. But he tries to look tough, like he imagines a killer would.

"So what do we do, chief?" one of the men asks.

"Krios said we keep order," says Chago. "So that's what we do."

"What was it like outside?" another one asks.

Chago shrugs.

"Green," he says.

The men look at each other in surprise.

"Green?"

"From plants."

"I'm dyin' to get out of here," says another man. "I want to get home."

"Me too," says another man. The others nod in agreement.

"If the prisoners are in charge, how come I'm more scared now than I was before?" says another man.

Chago realizes something. These men are no more devoted to Krios than he is.

"Listen," he says. "You wouldn't get ten feet out the gate before JustiCorps got you. They've got this place surrounded. They have ten times as many guns. They're just waiting for an excuse to blow us all away."

The men look at each other nervously.

"Well, what do we do then?" says one. "If JustiCorps doesn't get us, Krios will. He's a lunatic, and all his followers are lunatics too. Look how many people they've killed."

"There's one thing we can do that will save us," says Chago.

"What's that?"

"We get Krios."

A thrill runs through the group. They draw closer.

"But how do we do that?" asks one of the men. "He's always protected. He's got two dozen fighters with him at all times. And those guys are tough."

"We can use one of those things," Chago says. "One of those Innocence Devices."

"But how? How do we get him to go through?"

"We hide it," says Chago. "Cover it somehow. So he doesn't know it's there. He walks through. It gets him. Zap. It's over."

The men look at him admiringly. They like his plan.

I'm such an idiot, thinks Chago. *Now I have to do it.*

TWELVE

Chago has discovered something else. His armband is like a magic passport. It allows him to do whatever he wants and go wherever he wants. This is how he and his men are able to take down one of the Innocence Devices and move it. No one questions them. Not even other Krios men.

They set it up under cover of darkness around the main gate leading into the Admin Building. The top floors of the building have been destroyed, but the bottom ones are still standing. There are still guards and their children being kept in there, Chago has learned. Krios has made good on his promise not to hurt the children. So far. But anyone who would have a woman shot in cold blood is capable of anything.

Jim-Jim is in there, Chago knows. He is dying to hold the boy, but he doesn't want to go in and see him. Not yet. If Krios knows he has a son in there, that's one more thing he can use against him. So he keeps it quiet.

Krios deserves whatever he has coming to him.

They stand the Device on end and hide it with rubble and junk as best they can. When they are done, you can't even see it unless you know it's there. The sides of the gate hide it perfectly. Finally, Chago decides it's good enough. The sun is coming up.

"We don't give it power until right before he goes through," Chago says. "Set up a lookout. We keep one man here at all times.

Whoever sees him coming, flip the switch. Then you wait."

"We could be waiting a very long time," says one of the men, whose name is Rory.

"Or we could get lucky," says another, tapping Chago on the shoulder. He points down the avenue.

Chago can hardly believe his eyes. Krios and several of his men are coming their way right now.

"Give it power now," he says. "The rest of you guys, act like you're guarding the building. Everything's normal."

The men scramble to do as they are told. Chago hears a nearly silent hum as the Device comes to life. He tries to act calm as Krios approaches.

"Well, I see you like your new job," says Krios to Chago. "It suits you."

"Yes, sir," says Chago.

"That's fine." He beckons Chago closer. "Remember that fear is your best friend," he whispers. "That's how you keep them in line."

Chago nods.

"Yes, sir," he says.

Krios smiles and pats him on the shoulder. Then he and his men walk through the doorway—and through the Device.

Nothing happens.

When Krios and his men are gone, the others turn to Chago.

"Great plan," says one.

"I don't understand," says Chago. "Why didn't it work?" Angrily he thinks, If it killed Binny, it should have killed him.

"I know why," says Rory.

The others turn to him.

"Because the Innocence Device is rigged," says Rory.

"You mean there is no computer in it?" says Chago.

"There's a computer, all right," says Rory. "But the Warden ordered it disabled."

"How do you know all this?"

"I'm the one who disabled it," Rory tells him. "I was a programmer on the outside."

"Then how does the Innocence Device work?" Chago asks.

Rory shakes his head.

"It's the most amazing thing I've ever seen," he says. "You go through, and it reads you. It can tell whether you did something because you had to or because you didn't know any better or because you were just bad. Somehow it knows the difference."

"So it's real? It really works?"

"Yeah, it's real. But like I said, you can disable it. And you can program it to work however you want."

"How come you're just telling me this now?" says Chago.

"I had to be sure you were the real deal," says Rory. "One of us. Not one of them."

"Now we have to find another way to get him to go through the Device," says Chago.

"Just leave it here. I can turn it on again. Krios will come back this way. He has to when he comes out," says Rory. "I just need access to the computer room in the Admin Building. That's where the controls are."

Chago nods.

"Okay. Go do it. And don't get caught."

Rory nods and heads into the Admin Building. Chago watches him go. He has no way of knowing whether Rory is trustworthy or not. But he realizes he's too tired to care. He's been running on adrenaline for a long time now. If he doesn't get some sleep, he is going to collapse.

"The rest of you stay here and make sure no one else uses this entrance," he says.

"Yes, sir," says one of the men.

Chago sees the way he and the others look at him. With respect. No one has ever looked at him that way before.

He goes back to the last place on earth anyone would think of looking for him, to his own little box on the very edge of the city. And there he sleeps for what feels like a hundred days.

THIRTEEN

The next morning, all Chago can think about is what Rory said to him about the Device. It can tell whether you did something because you had to or because you were bad. All this time he has wondered if there is a difference. He doesn't believe he was born a criminal. Prison just made him into one.

He thinks back to a time long ago, a time he forced himself to forget. He had just arrived here in the city. The younger kids like him were easy marks for the older, tougher kids. They used to take his food or clothes.

Sometimes they beat him up for fun. And sometimes they did even worse things.

There was one boy, bigger than all the rest. He terrorized everyone. Chago forced himself to forget the boy's name. He knows he could remember it now if he tried. But he doesn't want to try.

Chago had decided to defend himself against this boy. He had been taking Chago's food every day. Chago was hungry, and he knew if he didn't eat soon, he was going to die. So he armed himself with a sharp piece of metal, and the next time the boy came around, he stuck it in his neck. Then he walked away.

There had been a lot of blood. It was the brightest red he'd ever seen.

He hadn't meant to kill him. He'd only meant to hurt him enough that he would think twice about ever coming near Chago again. But Chago heard later that the boy died shortly afterward.

About this he felt nothing. It wasn't wrong. It wasn't right. It was just a thing he had to do to survive.

Everyone knew Chago did it but the guards. And no one told on him. They were all glad. That boy had hurt a lot of other boys.

He wonders now if the Device could see this about him. And if it could, how would it judge him? Would it understand that he had to do it? Or would it decide that he should be killed?

Never mind, he thinks. I gave up thinking about that a long time ago. Wasn't wrong. Wasn't right. Just a thing I did to survive.

He thinks instead about Jim-Jim.

Today I am going to find my son, he says to himself. And there is not a force on earth that can stop me.

He takes up his gun as though he's been carrying it his whole life. He walks back through the streets to the Admin Building. On the way there he notices that no one speaks to him. But it's not because they don't see him. He can tell people are looking at him, even whispering about him. It's because they are showing him the highest sign of respect it is possible to show in this overcrowded world. They are giving him space. They move out of his way.

Must be the armband, he thinks. A little symbol can speak big things.

At the gates to the Admin Building he finds his men. When he shows up, they all look at him, waiting for him to speak.

"Well?" he says. "What's going on?"

"Rory got it working," says one of the men.

"And?"

"Krios and the others went through last night."

"So what happened?"

The man nods in the direction of a tarp. It's bright blue, and it covers something. Another man pulls back one corner. There Chago sees several bodies. Krios and his men. Now that he's dead, he's just another body. Death comes for everyone. There is something almost comforting about it. It may be the only thing he knows for sure. Chago just stares. Could it really have been this easy?

"Why didn't you come tell me right away?"

The men look at each other.

"No one wanted to bother you," says one.

Chago nods.

"So that's it," he says. "Who else knows about this?"

"Everyone seems to know," says Rory. "Everyone is saying you're the one who killed Krios. In their eyes, that means you run the city now."

"Me, run the city?"

The men nod. They look at him and wait. Chago realizes they are waiting for him to tell them what to do. He would like to tell them all to put down their guns and go home. But he knows it's too late for that.

"Where are the children?" he asks.

"We found them. They're all right. They're going to bring them out soon."

Chago feels like weeping with relief. But he forces himself to remain in control. He has to look tough.

"Where is the Warden?"

"He's locked up in the Admin Building."

"Bring him out," says Chago.

Some men go into the building and come out with the Warden. He's still wearing the same suit he had on when he appeared on the big screen. That seems like a thousand years ago.

"Who are you?" says the Warden. He doesn't look like he's in charge anymore. He just looks scared.

"My name doesn't matter," says Chago. "I'm just a prisoner. Same as everyone else here."

The Warden nods. He seems to know what's coming. He doesn't look scared yet. He just looks resigned.

"I had no choice," he says. "I had to do what I did. I'm just as trapped in this system as you are."

"What do you mean?" says Chago.

"You think I can just do what I want because I'm the Warden. I can't. I have masters too," says the Warden. "There were too many of you. Conditions were getting bad. Starvation, death-row fever. We had to bring the population down."

"You rigged it," says Chago. "You could have just let it work the way it was supposed to."

"If we did that, it would have killed everyone," says the Warden. "You're all monsters. All of you."

Chago says nothing to that. He just looks at him. These are the last words of a condemned man. He will let him say what's on his mind.

"So we gave people a chance at being free. We gave them hope. That's more than they had in a very long time," says the Warden.

"The problem with the system isn't the system. The problem is the people inside it," says Chago. "You should have stood up for what you knew was right."

"What do you mean?"

"How many shares do you own in JustiCorps?" asks Chago.

The Warden stares at him blankly.

"Go on, tell me. How many? A hundred? A thousand?"

The Warden swallows.

"Fifty thousand," he says.

"Fifty thousand shares. That means every time a prisoner is committed here, you make how much? Five bucks a year? Ten?"

"More like fifty," says the Warden.

Chago looks around.

"Does everybody hear that? He made money from us being locked up. Fifty dollars per man, per year. He must be a millionaire by now. You must have millions of dollars. Am I right? Are you a rich man?"

The Warden nods.

"Yes," he says. "Very rich. I could pay you all if...if you would just let me go."

Chago's men laugh at this. They laugh long and loud.

"Man," says Chago. "That's the funniest thing I've heard in a long time."

The Warden doesn't laugh.

"All right, Warden, I'm giving you the same chance you claimed to give us. The Device is working the way it's supposed to. If you really are innocent, then today is your lucky day. You know how it works. What do you think your chances are?"

The Warden doesn't answer.

"Come on, Warden. We want to hear what you have to say. Do you really believe you're a good man?"

"It's like the story of the Flood," the Warden says. "This had to happen. All of it. The wicked must be cleansed from the face of the earth. This is the way God wants it."

"You might just be right about that," says Chago.

FOURTEEN

Chago is about to order the Warden through the Device. But then something catches his eye, and he looks up. A handful of women are leading a large group of children out of the Admin Building. They blink in the bright light.

He sees Jim-Jim among them. An older boy is holding his hand. Chago feels relief wash over him. His boy is alive.

"Jim-Jim!" he calls. "It's me!"

Hearing his voice, the boy looks around for him. When their eyes meet, a feeling like he's never known washes over Chago.

Someday he will have to explain to the boy what happened to his mother. How he tried his best to save her but couldn't.

At least they will have each other.

"So you have a son," says the Warden. "I have a son too."

"Shut up," says Chago.

At that moment he hears a familiar clattering sound overhead. He looks up as a shadow crosses the earth.

Airships. Three of them. One is directly overhead.

"Attention, inmates," comes a voice. "You have one minute to lay down your weapons and surrender. Otherwise, we are going to destroy this city and everyone in it."

Everyone freezes. Then they look at Chago.

Chago thinks about what he could do. He could point his gun at the airships and start firing. This would do nothing, but it would mean fighting to the end, at least.

He could lay down his gun and surrender. But they would surely kill him sooner or later. He doesn't want to be a prisoner anymore.

But he does neither of these things. Something else in him takes over. He sees his little boy on the other side of the courtyard, and all he wants is to hold him in his arms and keep him safe. That is what a father is supposed to do. Chago didn't make the world he brought this boy into. But he can at least do all he can to protect him from it.

So he throws down his gun. Then he runs for his boy.

Too late, he remembers. The Device.

He has just passed through it.

He closes his eyes and waits for the flash of light.

EPILOGUE

When he thinks about those days, which is almost never, he can't even remember how much time has passed. Time seems to be playing tricks on him lately. He can look at his whole life and it seems to have taken no longer than the stroke of a bee's wing. Or he can look at the moment he is in, and it seems to stretch on for an eternity. Moments never end. But lives are over practically before they start. He will never understand the way time works. The only thing he knows about it is that it goes on whether he wants it to or not.

One thing he does understand is that he is not a prisoner anymore. He's free. He can do whatever he wants. He can be anywhere he wants. It's a feeling he's never known before.

But all Chago really wants to do is watch Jim-Jim.

He's not a little boy any longer. He has grown up to be a happy and healthy young man. Sometimes he looks like Corazon. Sometimes he looks like Chago. Sometimes he looks like himself.

Jim-Jim has a wife of his own now. A baby is on the way. He has escaped the clutches of JustiCorps. He is free. He will always be free.

Jim-Jim is so busy with his life that Chago doesn't know if he ever stops to think about him or not. He doesn't care. Jim-Jim seems to remember nothing of what happened to him when he was a child. For that, Chago is grateful.

Since the riot in the prison city, the world is a different place. No more money for prisoners. No more laws made by the rich to punish the poor. The world is not perfect, but it's better. People can begin to live freely again. The guilty have been brought to justice. Some of them anyway. There will always be dangerous people in the world. But you can't worry about them, Chago thinks. You can't live your life in fear. All you can do is live from one moment to the next. Be grateful for what you have. Worry about things when they happen, and not before.

Chago remembers when he used to believe that all of life was a prison, no matter where you turned. He can see now that this is not true. Even the greatest prison city in the world is temporary. It may seem like forever, but when it's done, you will see that it was nothing but the stroke of a bee's wing. Freedom is forever. And nothing can change that.

The Innocence Device is **WILLIAM KOWALSKI'S** fifth title in the Rapid Reads series (*The Barrio Kings, The Way It Works, Something Noble, Just Gone*). Kowalski is also an adult-education consultant, specializing in delivering curriculum to adults who are unemployed, under-educated and struggling to survive. He lives with his family in Nova Scotia.

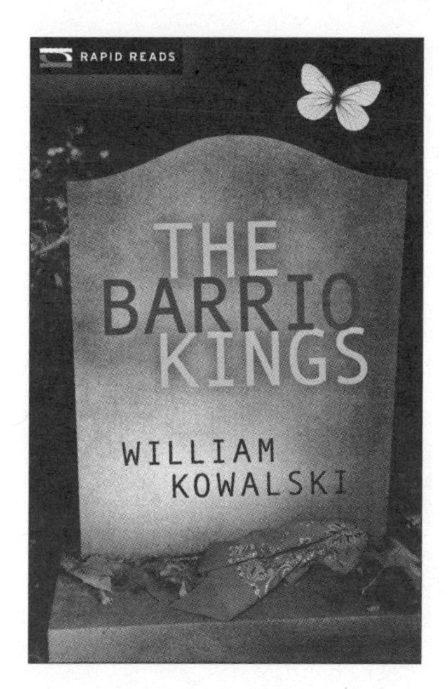

2011 Golden Oak Award Nominee
2011 SLJ's Top Book Choices for Youth in Detention List

Rosario Gomez gave up gang life after his brother was killed in a street fight. Now all he wants to do is finish night school and be a good father. But when an old friend shows up to ask him why he left the gang, Rosario realizes he was fooling himself if he thought his violent past would just go away.

"While the story can be seen as a cautionary tale about the dangers of gang life, it's never preachy...Recommended." —CM Magazine

Walter Davis is young, handsome, intelligent, dynamic and personable. Walter is also homeless. The medical expenses that came with his mother's brief and unsuccessful battle against cancer have left him destitute. Still, ever the optimist, Walter believes that if he lives in his car for a few months, he will have the time he needs to find a good job and turn his life around.

"With rare voices and taut suspense, these titles provide accessible choices for struggling and strong readers alike." —Booklist

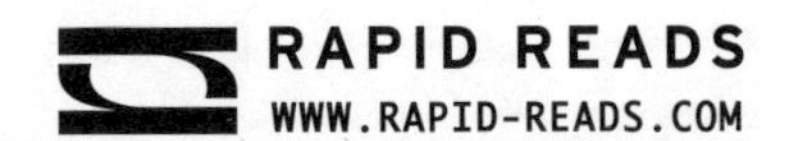